OHIO
DOMINICAN
UNIVERSITY™

SINCE 1911

OHIO DOMINICAN UNIVERSITY

1216 SUNBURY ROAD

COLUMBUS, OHIO 43219-2099

CALLAWAY

New York 2000

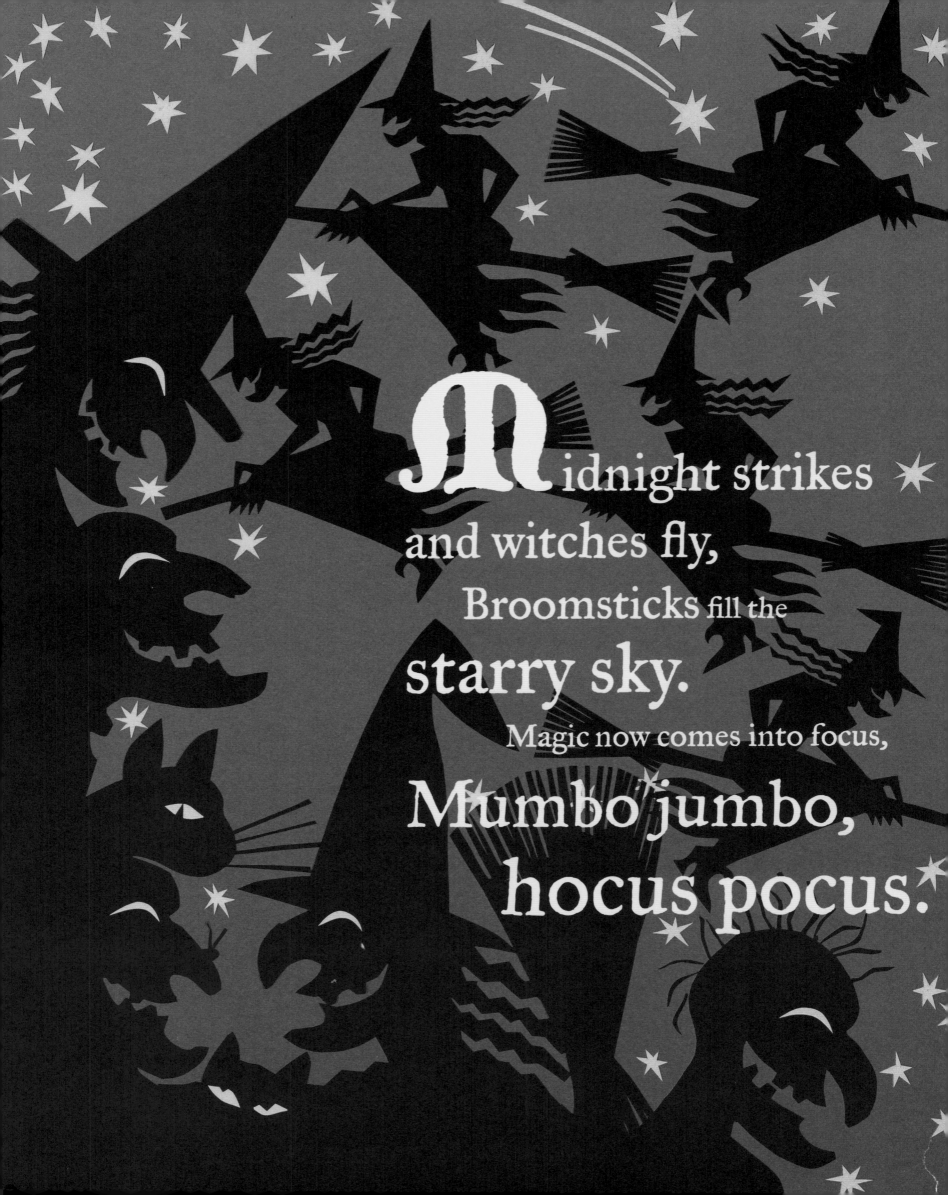

Midnight strikes
and witches fly,
Broomsticks fill the
starry sky.
Magic now comes into focus,
Mumbo jumbo,
hocus pocus.

Spells are made with
midnight's chime,
Magic poems set in rhyme.
Cauldrons thick with
lizard gumbo,
Hocus pocus,
mumbo jumbo.

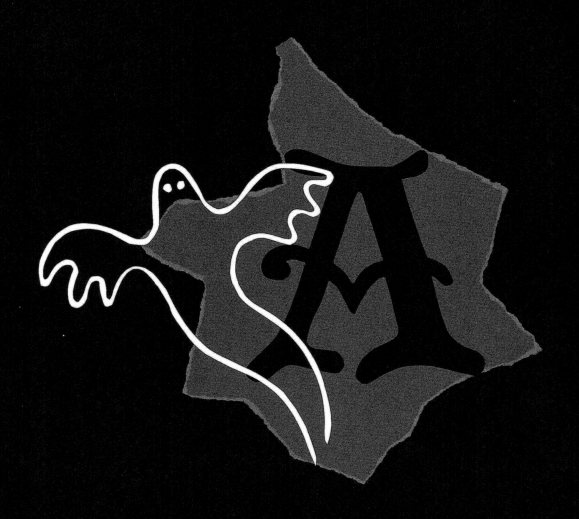

Abracadabra, a conjurer's cat
Was peppered with **stars** flying out of a hat.

"Not the dish that I wished,"

He thought as he sat.

"I wanted a **fish with some
french fries and rat.**"

Bats go flapping
in the **night,**
Turning left,
turning **right.**
Swirling high
above the **town,**
Bored with hanging
upside down.

Cobwebs in the attic,

More webs in the hall.

Cobwebs on the stairway,

Clinging to the wall.

Cobwebs in the dungeon,

Stretched from arch to arch.

What a lot of websites

For spiders on the march.

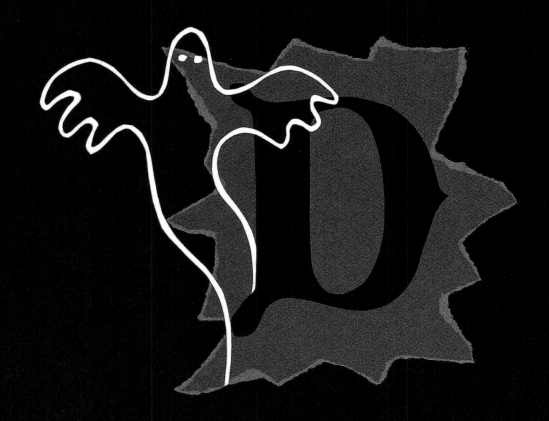

When dragons choke,
They sneeze out smoke
And cough up sparks——
It's not a joke.

If flu affects
Your local dragon,
Be sure to drive
A fireproof wagon.

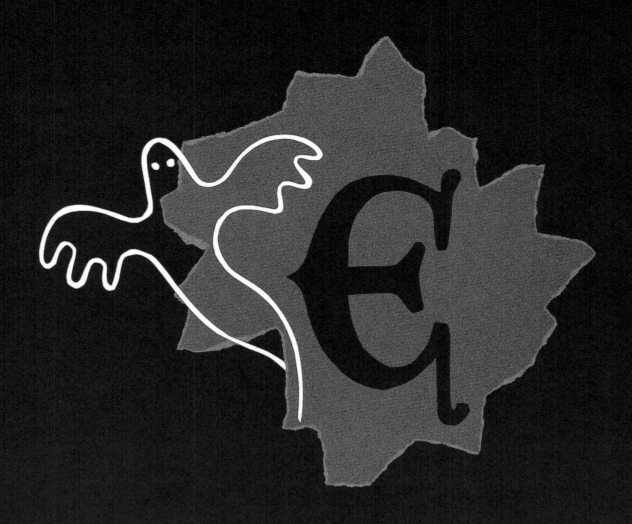

To make a quite

disgusting brew,

Throw some

eyeballs in a stew.

Serve with carrot, bean, or leek.

This will see you

through the week.

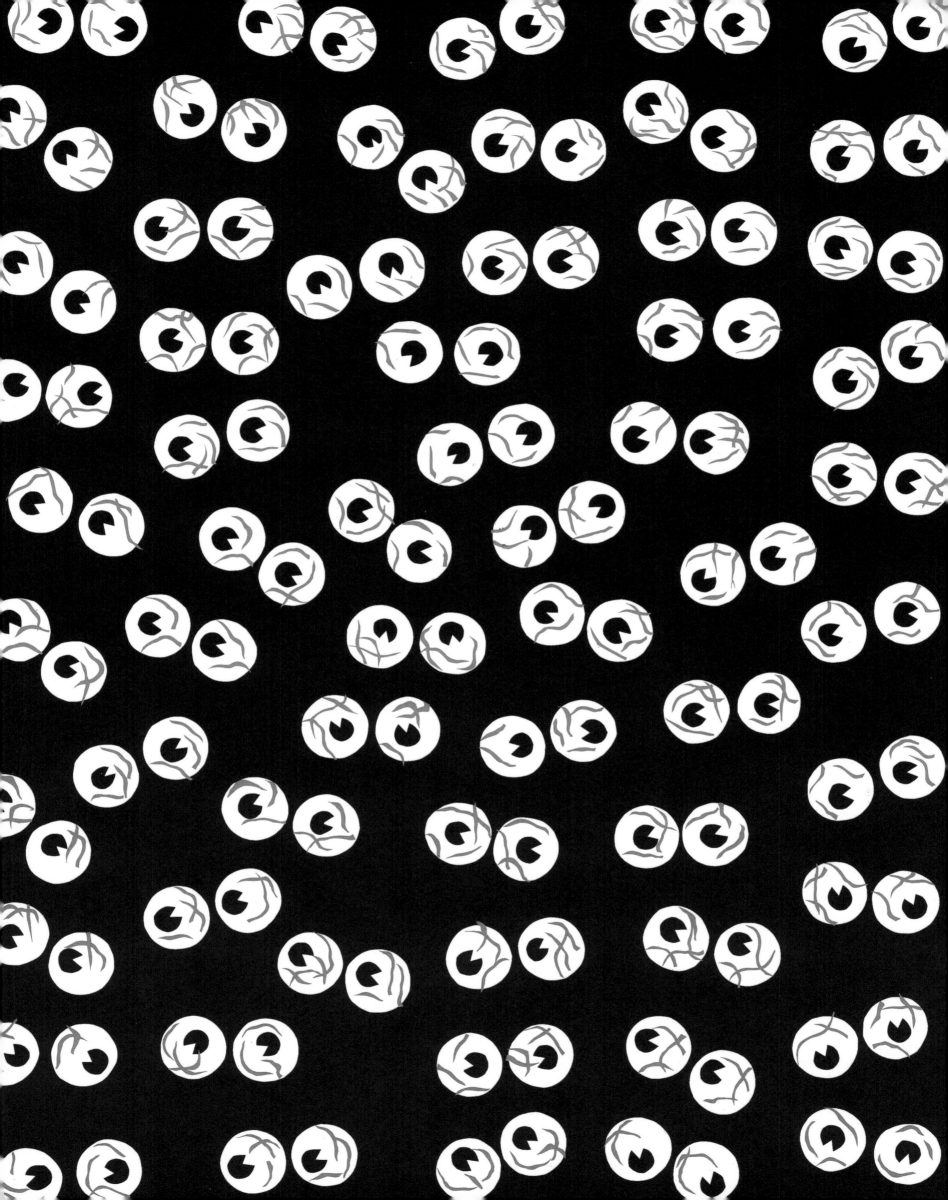

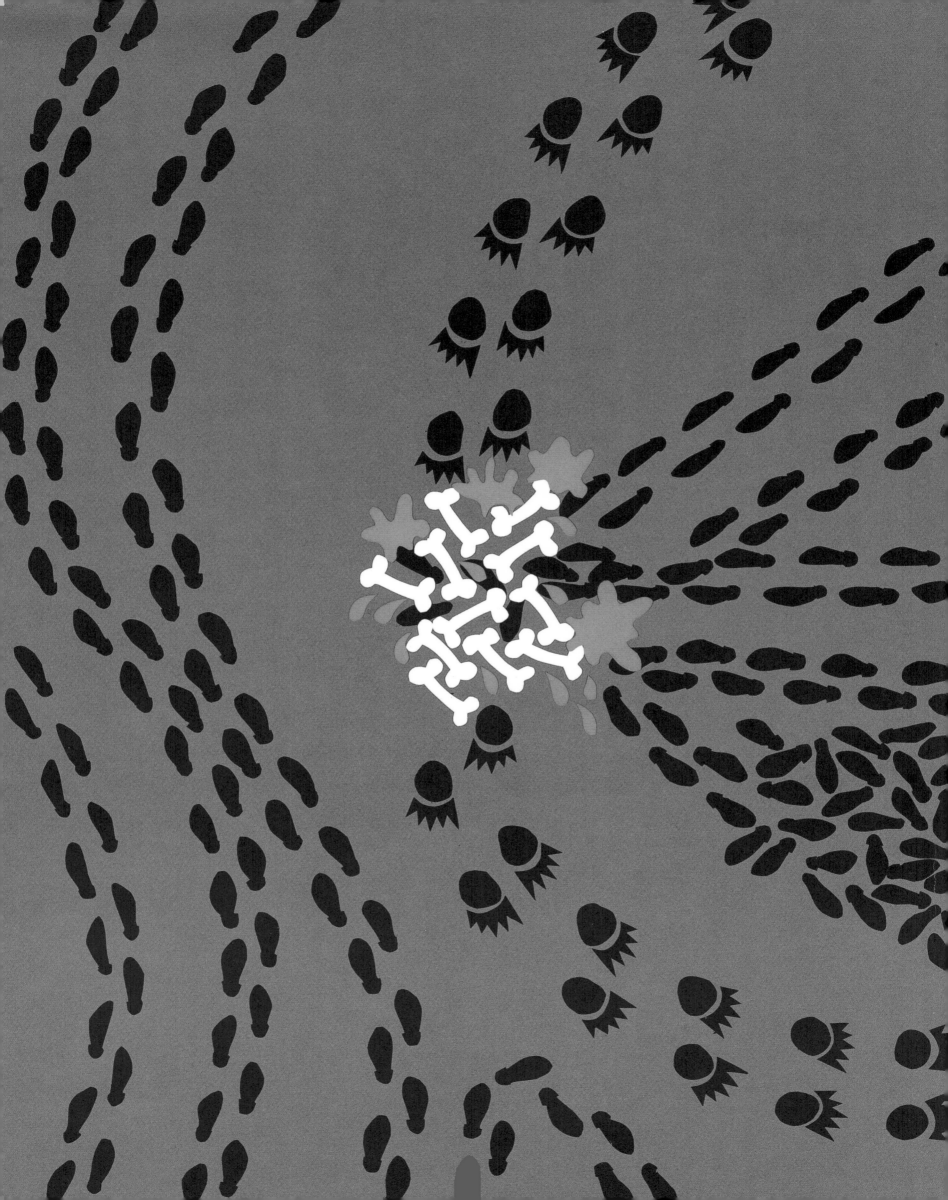

I saw some **footprints** on a track,

Muddled footprints,

some turned **back.**

I saw some **bones**

and understood,

Bears aren't friendly
in this wood.

The **mist** that
shivers on the river
Holds a secret if you peek.
Phantom figures
quake and quiver——
Ghosts are playing
hide and seek.

A sneaky-looking harlequin

Smiled and said as he crept in,

"I've come to steal——I love nice stuff——

Bright jeweled things, can't get enough.

Yes, diamonds are my favorite loot,

You must have guessed it by my suit."

So did the cops, who weren't impressed.

They caught him thanks to how he's dressed.

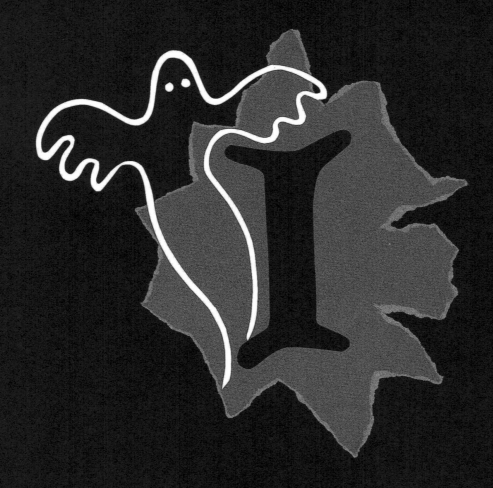

An **imp** is

a silly

tiny creature.

Dancing is its

finest feature.

A **king** who lost his sense of humor

Called for help——well, that's the rumor,

And summoning his heads of court

Said, "I'm so sad, I feel distraught.

I need a life with laughter in it.

Go and get me **Jester** Minute.

He'll make me smile, that's beneficial.

I'll give him treasure, that's official.

But if he makes me frown instead,

Then," said the king, **"Off with his head."**

A **knight** by day is full of stress,

Saving damsels in distress,

**Righting wrongs
and doing good,**

Slaying dragons in the wood.

But all this action leaves him dead.

The weekend finds him ill in bed,

Too tired to be a **disco diva**

Or for **Saturday knight fever.**

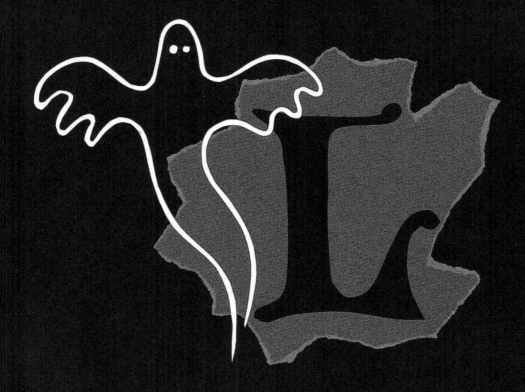

A genie stuck inside a lamp

Can often get a painful cramp,

And after squeezing

through the spout,

Is very mad

when he's let out.

If your genie's

looking mean,

It isn't wise to call him Gene.

There must be a hieroglyphic
for a person so terrific.

She's Egyptian, she's not crummy,

my three-thousand-year-old mummy.

Some might say she's most alarming,

I have always found her charming.

Who do I long to be nearest?

Dusty, musty

Mummy Dearest.

When darkness falls and you're in bed,
Nightmares come as clear as day.
Monsters crawl inside your head.

You run but just can't get away.

You **fly**, you **fall**, you **often scream.**

You do things, **most of which aren't cool.**

But when you wake it's just a dream,

And then you really feel a **fool.**

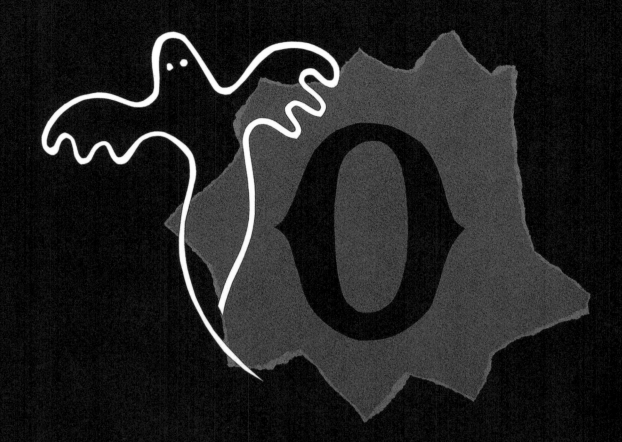

An ogre

(something like a giant)

Becomes confused

if you're **defiant.**

And if you throw him out of town,

Panicking he'll knock you down.

But even though they're scary guys

Most ogres will apologize.

They know that life is **not so sweet**

When you get **squashed by ten-ton feet.**

Pumpkin man,
pumpkin man,
Doesn't have a
dental plan.
Will he soon be that much wiser

Now he's lost his

right incisor?

Playing in the sand is great,

But some of us can't **celebrate**.

Like those who accidentally choose

To play on sand that starts to **ooze**.

They thought the **quicksand** looked appealing.

Now they've got that **sinking feeling**.

Never make a **raven** mad——

His temper is extremely bad.

He also can——and this is worse——

Zap you with a **nasty curse.**

Perhaps you think this isn't so?

Just ask the guy who called him **"crow."**

The raven turned him into straw,

Then flew off squawking, "Nevermore."

Sorcerers who **stand** and **shriek**

Often find their **spells** are weak.

Wizards who cannot orate

See their **spells** disintegrate.

To make a **spell** that can't be broken,

Magic must be clearly spoken.

If you simply stand and mumble,

Serves you right if it's a jumble.

Here's a tale, the saddest fable,

About a witch called Munching Mabel,

Famed for cooking stuff delicious,

Truly tasty, most nutritious.

One day she thought she had to try

To bake a magic mushroom pie.

So off she ran to woods to find

Mushrooms of the perfect kind.

Alas, poor Mabel [nice but slow]

Stopped right there where toadstools grow.

And quite forgetting in her haste

Their very deadly poisoned taste,

Picked the biggest, white and red,

Then munching on it, fell down...

A **unicorn**

has just one horn.

That's magic.

A horse

has none, of course.

That's tragic.

The **vampire** is no good
at **saving**
Blood for which he's
always craving.
When no blood is in the **bank he**
Ends up feeling very
cranky.

Beware of **wolves**
with hungry eyes.
They often turn up in disguise,
Searching for a **tasty snack**
(Something bigger than **Big Mac**).
With cunning makeup they pretend
To be a **neighbor** or a **friend,**
And, I've even heard it said
A wolf was found in grandma's bed.
To me it's easy how to **spot**
Who's a wolf and who is **not.**
A person's teeth are not so big;
A wolf's more hairy, wears a **wig.**

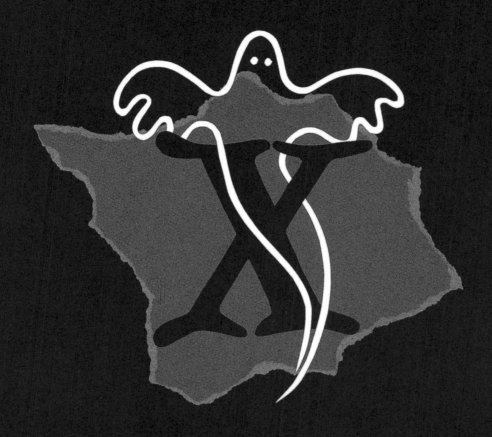

Oh, how I wish for

X-ray eyes

To catch my victims by **surprise,**

To take a look inside their clothes

And see the secrets no one knows.

The only problem with this game?

All **skeletons** look much the **same.**

I met a yeti
in Tibet.
Took him home
to be a pet.
Ate my friends
and family.
Think he's saving
me for tea.

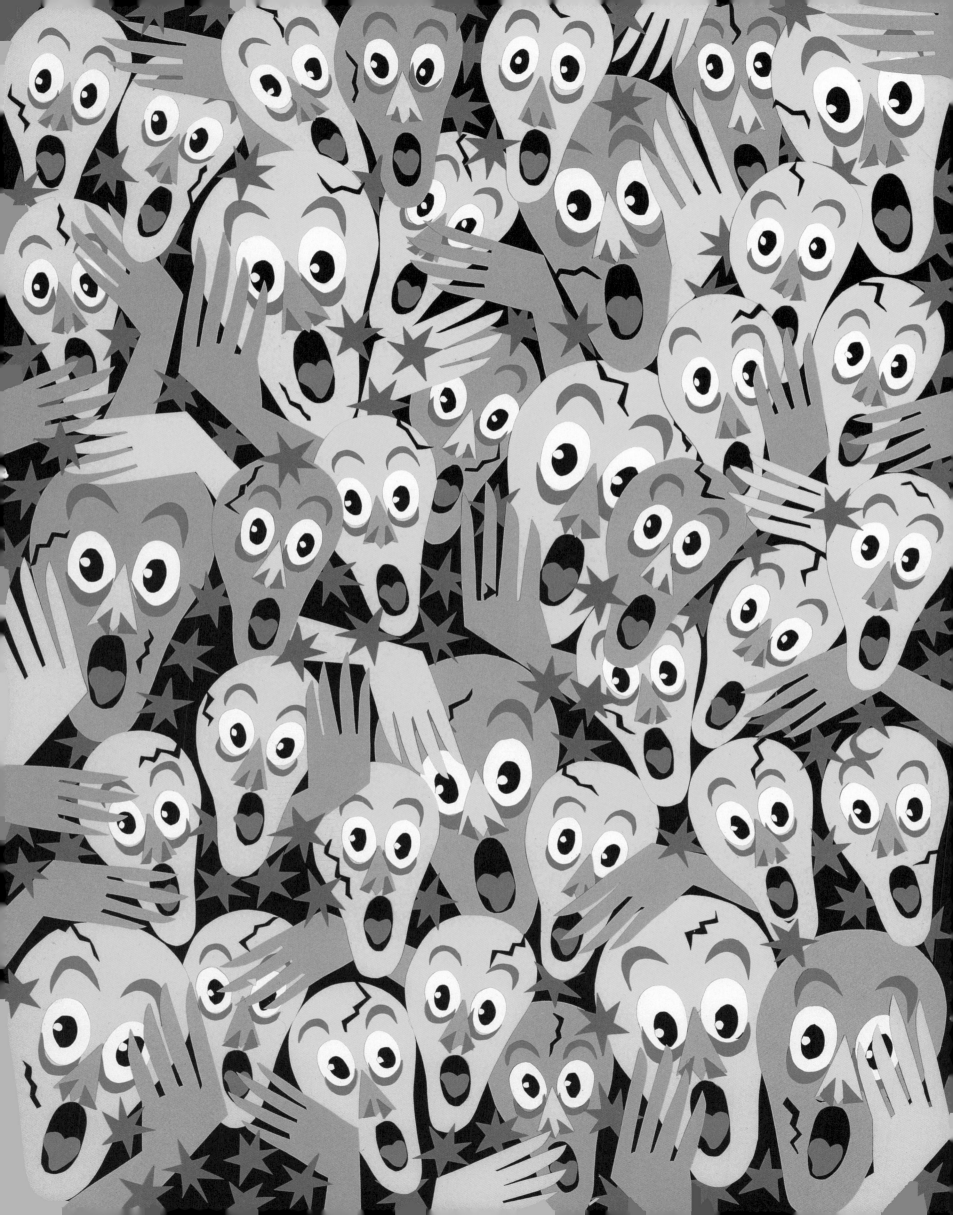

Zombies fill
me with misgiving,
Should be dead but still are living,
Looking bad with
red eyes warning———,
Just like I look
in the morning.

About the Author

After dazzling readers with his first book, *The Jungle ABC*, Michael Roberts——the scissors-wielding
wizard of snip——returns in *Mumbo Jumbo* with some sinister companions. Roberts, who is currently the
Visual Fashion Director of *The New Yorker* magazine, has also been art director of *Tatler*, Paris editor
of *Vanity Fair*, and contributing editor of *Condé Nast Traveler*.

His writing, illustrations, and photographs have appeared in *GQ*,
Esquire, Harpers & Queen, and *The New Yorker*.

Roberts lives in Paris.

Callaway
64 Bedford Street
New York, NY 10014

Printed in China by Palace Press International

First Edition

10 9 8 7 6 5 4 3 2 1

ISBN 0-935112-49-9
Library of Congress Catalog Card Information Available

Editor-in-Chief: Nicholas Callaway   Editor: Edward Brash   Associate Publisher: Paula Litzky
Director of Production: True Sims   Art Director & Designer: Jennifer Wagner   Assistant Editor: Christopher Steighner

DATE DUE

APR 29 2003				
NOV 17 2003				
⌐ ⌐ 5 '85				
JAN 25 '85				